UNDERCOVER BOOKWORMS

Don't miss any of the cases in the Hardy Boys Clue Book series!

HARDY BOYS

→ Clue Book ←

#16

UNDERCOVER BOOKWORMS

BY FRANKLIN W. DIXON ⇆ ILLUSTRATED BY SANTY GUTIÉRREZ

ALADDIN
NEW YORK   LONDON   TORONTO   SYDNEY   NEW DELHI

ALADDIN

An imprint of Simon & Schuster Children's Publishing Division
1230 Avenue of the Americas, New York, New York 10020
First Aladdin paperback edition June 2023
Text copyright © 2023 by Simon & Schuster, Inc.
Illustrations copyright © 2023 by Santy Gutiérrez
THE HARDY BOYS, HARDY BOYS CLUE BOOK, and colophons are registered trademarks of Simon & Schuster, Inc.
Also available in an Aladdin hardcover edition.
All rights reserved, including the right of reproduction in whole or in part in any form.
ALADDIN and related logo are registered trademarks of Simon & Schuster, Inc.
THE HARDY BOYS and colophons are registered trademarks of Simon & Schuster, Inc.
HARDY BOYS CLUE BOOK and colophons are trademarks of Simon & Schuster, Inc.
For information about special discounts for bulk purchases, please contact Simon & Schuster Special Sales at 1-866-506-1949 or business@simonandschuster.com.
The Simon & Schuster Speakers Bureau can bring authors to your live event.
For more information or to book an event contact the Simon & Schuster Speakers Bureau at 1-866-248-3049 or visit our website at www.simonspeakers.com.
Series designed by Karina Granda
Cover designed by Alicia Mikles
Interior designed by Mike Rosamilia
The illustrations for this book were rendered digitally.
The text of this book was set in Adobe Garamond Pro.
0523 OFF
2 4 6 8 10 9 7 5 3 1
Library of Congress Cataloging-in-Publication Data
Names: Dixon, Franklin W., author. | Gutiérrez, Santy, 1971- illustrator.
Title: Undercover bookworms / by Franklin W. Dixon ; illustrated by Santy Gutierrez.
Description: First Aladdin paperback edition. | New York : Aladdin, 2023. | Series: Hardy Boys clue book ; #16 | Audience: Ages 6 to 9. | Summary: Detective brothers Frank and Joe must catch a book thief to save their library.
Identifiers: LCCN 2023007135 (print) | LCCN 2023007136 (ebook) | ISBN 9781534476868 (pbk) | ISBN 9781534476875 (hc) | ISBN 9781534476882 (ebook)
Subjects: CYAC: Libraries—Fiction. | Rare books—Fiction. | Stealing—Fiction. | Brothers—Fiction. | Mystery and detective stories. | BISAC: JUVENILE FICTION / Mysteries & Detective Stories | JUVENILE FICTION / Action & Adventure / General | LCGFT: Detective and mystery fiction. | Novels.
Classification: LCC PZ7.D644 Un 2023 (print) | LCC PZ7.D644 (ebook) | DDC [Fic]—dc23
LC record available at https://lccn.loc.gov/2023007135
LC ebook record available at https://lccn.loc.gov/2023007136

CONTENTS

CONTENTS

Chapter 1

SHHHHHHH!

"Just one more," eight-year-old Joe Hardy encouraged his older brother, Frank.

Joe picked up a thick volume of classic detective stories and climbed onto the step stool.

"I don't know, Joe." Frank's voice quivered. So did the impossibly tall stack of books he was trying to carry through the mystery section of the Bayport Junior Public Library.

"Don't give up now, bro." Joe gently placed the

book atop the teetering stack. "I think this is a world record."

"I'm less worried about breaking records than returning these to the shelves so I can get to the rest of my Junior Librarian duties." Frank took a cautious step forward. "How am I supposed to see where I'm going?"

Frank was a summer volunteer at the Bayport Junior Public Library—or BJPL for short—and he was determined to do a good job. Joe was taking a break from reading comics to help out. Sort of.

"Teamwork!" Joe said. "Just like when we solve a mystery. We're the best kid detectives in all of Bayport. We've cracked some of the toughest cases in town. Putting a few books back should be a cinch. Now just follow my voice."

"Okay," Frank replied uncertainly from behind the swaying tower of books.

"The author of this one is Victor Appleton, so let's head for the *A*s." Joe marched confidently down the aisle. "This way!"

Frank took a slow step forward. Only his foot

didn't land on the library's worn-down carpet. It smacked right into another step stool instead. Frank fell forward, and so did the books.

"Ahhhhhh!" he cried as a tsunami of paperbacks and hardcovers swept over Joe.

"Whoops," Joe uttered, now standing amid a messy pile of books. "I guess that last book was the mystery that broke the detectives' stack."

"What in the world is going on here?!" a woman's voice demanded from the end of the aisle.

Harriet Porter had blond hair, round wire-rimmed glasses, and a BJPL T-shirt with a picture of a worm reading a book. The worm had glasses just like hers.

"I'm sorry, boss," Frank said to the head librarian. "Joe was helping me put the returned books back, but I tried to carry too many at once."

Harriet stared wide-eyed at the books scattered all over the floor.

Joe gave her a guilty smile. "Sorry."

"Why are you carrying them by hand in the first place?" the librarian asked Frank.

"The cart's broken," Frank said.

She groaned. "Again?"

Frank nodded. "Marni is using the other one."

He pointed to a middle school girl in a Winnie-the-Pooh costume pushing a loaded cart past the end of the aisle. Marni loved to cosplay famous book characters, and she always showed up in a different costume. The boys could hear the cart's loose wheel clunking with every rotation, making it sound like a wobbly shopping cart.

"I think it might be time for an upgrade," Joe suggested.

"We can barely afford to keep fixing the rusty old antiques we have. Forget about getting new ones." Harriet took off her glasses and rubbed the bridge of her nose. "How does the town council expect us to keep things running smoothly when they won't even put enough money in the budget for basic equipment or maintenance?"

"Hopefully lots of people will show up for the council meeting tomorrow night to show their

support." Frank nodded toward the front of the library, where a sign stood beside the checkout desk. It read:

THE BAYPORT BOOKWORMS NEED YOU!
SIGN THE PETITION & TELL THE TOWN
COUNCIL TO SUPPORT THE JUNIOR
PUBLIC LIBRARY!

Next to the poster, right behind the desk, was a large aquarium. It wasn't filled with water, though. It was filled with dirt. And instead of fish, it was crawling with the library's mascots—real live worms!

"If things don't go well at the meeting, I don't know what we'll do." Harriet twisted her hands together. "This is the only library branch in the whole region devoted just to children's literature and kids. If they cut the budget any more, we might have to close a few days a week, and that would be a loss for the whole community."

"They can't cut the budget!" Joe glanced around the busy library. There were kids of all ages reading,

using the computers, and doing lots of other activities. Some of them were hand-painting their own SUPPORT THE LIBRARY signs. "This is one of the best hangouts around."

"I sure hope you're right," the librarian said. "We provide an important service for Bayport's kids, but we don't make money for the town, and some of the council members care more about that than books." She sighed deeply. "Or kids."

"It will work out," Frank insisted. "It's got to!"

"Too bad you boys aren't on the town council." Harriet picked a book up off the floor and handed it to Frank. "Go ahead and get this mess cleaned up. I'm going to try fixing that other cart—"

Before she could finish, there was a commotion in the quiet reading section at the back of the library.

"That doesn't sound very quiet—" Joe started to say, but he was interrupted too. By someone screaming!

ROBED RUCKUS

Harriet ran toward a bright, bold sign at the back of the library that read QUIET CORNER. The boys were right behind her.

"Gandalf is clearly the best wizard!" a boy in a burgundy robe shouted across one of the tables at a girl in a Bayport Elementary School Environment Club T-shirt.

The girl looked at him over the top of a large book about tree identification and shrugged. "Sorry,

Jeff, I'm team Merlin. Although Dumbledore is pretty cool too."

"What?!" Jeff shrieked.

"Shhhhh!" Marni rushed over, holding a finger up to her lips. "This is the quiet reading area."

"I'm not going to *shhhhh* until Kitty admits who the world's the top wizard is," Jeff insisted loudly.

"You want to know who the top wizard in this library is?" Harriet interrupted, jabbing a ballpoint pen in Jeff's direction. "Me, and if you don't quiet down this instant, I'm going to wave my magic wand and make you disappear." The librarian whirled her pen in the air and pointed at the front door. "Right out of the building."

Jeff hung his head and pulled the robe tighter around himself. It looked a lot like a wizard's robe, only instead of a crest, there was a patch with the Bayport Bookworm logo on the chest. The words REIGNING READER were stitched below it in gold thread.

"This is the second time I've had to warn you, Jeff," Harriet said sternly. "Just because you earned the right to wear the Reading Robe doesn't mean you get to ignore the rules. I expect more out of my Reigning Readers."

Every week, the kid who read the most books got to wear the Reading Robe. There were actually a few robes in different sizes to make sure each Reigning Reader had a robe that fit, but Harriet only ever gave out one at a time. Frank had worn the robe proudly a few times, but Jeff had been the Reigning Reader for three straight weeks, a BJPL record.

"I just get really excited about the characters I like," Jeff explained.

"If you think he gets worked up about wizards, don't even get him started on elves," Kitty warned as she tucked her book under her arm and stood up. "Yesterday he picked a fight with the entire Keeper of the Lost Cities fan club." She pointed up at the QUIET CORNER sign and walked off. "I'm going to find a quieter corner to read in."

Harriet rubbed her eyes. "I appreciate your passion for literary debate, Jeff, but yelling at people who disagree with you isn't acceptable. One more strike, and you're out of the library for an entire week."

Everyone gasped. Harriet almost never kicked anyone out.

"I'm sorry, Harriet," Jeff said meekly. "I'll do better."

"What's all the ruckus?" a deep voice asked.

When the boys looked up, they saw a man with a

neatly trimmed goatee. He had on a nice button-down shirt and was carrying a leather briefcase. A black-and-white toy poodle poked its head out of a pocket on the side.

"Hey, Councilman Tom," Harriet greeted the man. "Sorry about the disturbance. Some of our readers can get a little *too* excited about books."

"Hi, Tom. Jeff Le Guin. Nice to meet ya!" Jeff rushed over with his hand outstretched. "I'm a big fan of your work on the town council."

Tom laughed and shook Jeff's hand. "A budding politician, I see."

Jeff nodded eagerly. He was the president of Joe's class at Bayport Elementary, and everyone at school knew he hoped to run for a real public office someday.

There was a sudden tiny growl from Tom's side.

When they looked down, the toy poodle was chewing furiously on a number 2 pencil.

"Put that down, Mulley," Tom said, taking the pencil from the poodle and scratching its head affectionately.

"Puppy!" Marni bounced up and down before turning to Tom. "Is it okay if I say 'hi'?"

"Go for it," Tom said. "She's a real people pup."

Marni knelt down to the briefcase and offered her hand for the little dog to sniff. "She has her own puppy pocket!"

"I had it custom made so she'd be able to go everywhere with me," Tom said. "I'm pretty sure Mulley is the most spoiled dog in Bayport."

"How's the library budget vote looking, Councilman?" Harriet asked cautiously.

Tom frowned. "That's actually what I came to tell you. You know that I and some of the other council members are big supporters of BJPL's mission, but the town is facing some tough budget decisions, and there are other projects that need money too."

"Not the golf course?" The librarian rolled her eyes.

"Upgrading the public golf course has a lot of support." Tom glanced across the room to the other side of the library, where Kitty had just reappeared, plopping into a torn but comfy oversize chair to read her tree book in peace. Kitty's mom, Bonnie Becker, was the town council president—and four-time champ of the local golf tournament. There had been lots of articles in the *Bayport Bugle* about how she and Kitty had won last year's adult and kid tournaments.

"A couple of key votes are still undecided, and

DYNAMIC MOTHER-DAUGHTER GOLF DUO

well—" Tom paused. "Some of the other council members don't think it's worth spending extra money to keep a separate library branch open when they already have a lot of the same books at the main library."

"But BJPL has some of the most popular educational programs around!" Frank exclaimed.

"And it gives kids a place to spend time when they're not in school!" Marni said, tugging on her Pooh ears.

"And you can never have enough books!" Jeff insisted, twisting the belt of his robe.

"All of the above and then some!" Joe added.

"I agree with all of you, and I'm going to do my best to help keep it that way, but—" Tom looked around the library and grimaced. "If the other council members saw how it looked in here, it would be hard to convince them."

"But how are we supposed to fix things and keep them nice when the council won't give us any money for maintenance?" Harriet protested.

"It's not just that," Tom said apologetically.

"There's nobody watching the front desk." Harriet bit her lip. "You can hear kids yelling from the sidewalk." Jeff looked down at his feet. "There are books all over the floor." This time it was Frank and Joe who looked down. "And even worse, the door to the Rare Reads room is wide open."

Harriet gasped, and both Jeff and Marni whimpered.

Rare Reads was a special locked room on the other side of the library that held BJPL's rarest, most valuable books and comics. The most prized—like a signed first edition of the world-famous children's book *Magical Moon*—were kept in locked glass display cases. Being let into the room to read was a special privilege. Rare Reads books couldn't be checked out like regular books, but kids who took a pledge to follow a strict set of rules were allowed to sign in to have the room unlocked so they could read inside. The two most important rules were to be super-duper careful with the books and to never, ever leave the room unattended.

"Anyone could walk right in," Tom continued.

"Those books are town property. That first edition of *Magical Moon* is worth a fortune. It was a big decision to let the BJPL keep a signed copy of one of the most famous books ever. If it got damaged or lost—" Tom sighed. "I hate to say this, but maybe they really would be safer at the main library."

Harriet narrowed her eyes at Marni. "Why is the door to Rare Reads open?"

Once a Junior Librarian graduated from

elementary school, Harriet gave them more responsibilities. The ones she trusted most, like Marni, even got to use the keys.

"It's not my fault!" Marni pointed at Jeff, who had gone pale. "He signed in to read *The Wild World of Wizarding*. I closed the door behind him, just like I'm supposed to."

Jeff froze in place with his mouth open. The door locked automatically and could only be opened without a key from the inside.

Harriet's narrowed eyes swung from Marni to Jeff. The librarian could get frustrated sometimes when kids misbehaved, but she was usually really good at keeping her cool. This time, though, she started turning red.

"You left the Rare Reads room door open to go pick a book fight with Kitty?"

"I, um, uh—" Jeff fumbled.

"Strike three!" she shouted like a major-league umpire. "You're out!"

"But—" Jeff didn't get a chance to finish.

"Get your things and go." The librarian aimed

her finger at the door. "But the robe stays."

Frank and Joe gasped, and Jeff's lip started quivering.

"Not the robe," he pleaded.

But Harriet wasn't backing down.

"The robe."

A tear fell from the corner of Jeff's eye and ran slowly down his cheek.

For the first time in the history of the Bayport Junior Public Library, the Reigning Reader had lost their robe.

Chapter
3

BOOK BANISHMENT

Jeff slowly removed the robe but couldn't bring himself to let go when Harriet tried to take it.

"Please," he begged.

"If you care about the library, you'll follow my rules, and you can come back next week." The librarian mumbled the next part under her breath. "If there's a library to come back to."

Jeff growled and ran robeless from the Quiet Corner, bumping into Tom as he fled. Mulley leaped from her puppy pocket and Tom's briefcase fell to the floor, spilling papers everywhere.

"You'll be sorry for this!" Jeff cried before disappearing from sight.

Harriet scrambled to help the councilman pick up his papers. "I'm so sorry, Tom. I promise nothing like this will happen again."

"That's actually why I'm here, unfortunately."

The serious tone in Tom's voice made Harriet stop and look up.

"I wanted to tell you in person, since we're friends. There's been a change to the agenda for the council meeting. We aren't just voting on whether to cut the junior library's budget. The vote is on whether to close it altogether."

"No!" the boys, Marni, and Harriet all blurted at the same time.

"But the junior library is a Bayport cultural landmark!" Frank exclaimed.

Tom frowned. "Nothing is decided yet, and I'm still going to fight for you, but it doesn't look good."

"You're not going to tell everyone about what happened with Jeff leaving the Rare Reads room open, are you?" Harriet asked hesitantly.

"I'm going to close the room up now!" Marni ran as quickly as she could from the Quiet Corner, calling back over her shoulder, "I'll never let anyone read a Rare Read unsupervised again, I promise!"

Tom watched Marni go, then turned back to

Harriet. "I'll do my best to soften the blow, but I have an obligation as an elected official to report what happened here to the council."

Harriet bit her lip. "But that could give Bonnie Becker all the reason she needs to convince the other council members to give the money to the golf course instead!"

"Don't give up, Harriet. There's still a chance." Tom tucked Mulley back into her puppy pocket. "I'm sorry we didn't come with happier news."

Frank and Joe stood by Harriet's side as she watched the councilman leave.

"The Bayport Junior Library is my whole life." Harriet's voice was barely a whisper. "I don't know what I'll do if they shut us down."

"It means a lot to all of us," Joe said.

"Half the kids in Bayport depend on it," Frank added. "They can't really shut it down, can they?"

"Even with Councilman Tom's support, we're going to have to pull off a miracle before the council meeting tomorrow night, or the junior library could be closed"—the librarian gulped—"forever."

They heard the jingle of the front door as Tom opened it to leave.

That wasn't the only thing they heard. There was another scream, this time from the direction of Rare Reads. Everyone turned, including Tom.

"Harriet!" Marni wailed. "Come quick! *Magical Moon!* It's gone!"

Chapter 4

CASE OPEN

Frank and Joe sprinted for the Rare Reads room alongside Harriet. When they got there, Jeff wasn't the only thing that was gone.

The room was small but cozy and filled with old books. Some of them were on shelves with their spines out like normal library books and some were displayed behind wall-mounted cases to show off their covers. In the center of the room was a reading table, around which stood three separate glass cases atop pedestals. They each had a little light inside like you might see shining down on a museum's most precious objects. There was a mint-condition classic superhero comic in the one on the left and a two-hundred-year-old book of fairy tales in the one on the right. The case in the middle had a light just like the other two, but the only thing illuminated by this one was empty space.

Marni stood in front of it with her eyes wide and her hands over her mouth.

Frank gawked at the empty case. "It's really gone!"

Magical Moon
Signed 1st edition

"How could this happen?" Harriet demanded.

Marni just shook her head. She looked like she was about to cry. "I'll—I'll go search the library. Maybe someone just took it out and moved it."

She ran out of the room as Tom walked in. His forehead was wrinkled with worry lines and he was yanking on his hair.

"You lost *Magical Moon*?! That first edition is one of the most valuable children's books in the entire public library system! This is terrible news. Come on, Mulley. We have to report this to the council right away."

Harriet moaned as the councilman rushed out of the library. "*Magical Moon* is gone—along with the junior library's future!"

Frank and Joe looked at each other and nodded. They knew a mystery when they saw one.

"*Magical Moon* may be gone for now, but we have a special rare book of our own." Joe pulled out a notebook. "The clue book!"

"*The Clue Book?*" Harriet asked. "I don't think we have that one in our catalog."

"That's because it's a one-of-a-kind Hardy boys original," Joe said.

"It's where we write down the Five Ws at the start of every case," Frank told the librarian. "Those are the questions we need to answer to solve any mystery. Who, wh—"

"What, where, when, and why." Harriet finished listing the Ws for him with a wink. "Don't forget, I'm a librarian. We know everything—" She suddenly buried her face in her hands. "Except how to save our own library! If we don't find *Magical Moon* fast, the town council will vote to close us for sure!"

"Not if we can help it," Frank said. "We're not just library lovers. We're also the top kid detectives in Bayport. This is the Case of the Missing Mystery, and solving it could also mean saving the library."

Joe clicked open his pen. "So we're gonna solve it!"

At the top of a blank page in the clue book, he wrote *The Case of the Missing Mystery*.

"Let's start with the questions we know the answers to for sure," Frank suggested. "*What* and *where*."

Joe wrote down *Magical Moon is missing* and *Rare Reads*.

Frank scratched his chin. "*When* gets a little trickier."

"I can tell you when it wasn't gone," Harriet interjected. "An hour ago when I walked by. Everything was locked up tight and in its right place."

Joe glanced up at the clock and wrote down *Between three p.m. and four p.m.*

"Which brings us right to *who*," Frank said as Joe wrote down the word *Suspects* in the clue book. "We know for a fact there was one *who* here *when*, and they also happen to have a *why*."

Joe instantly started writing a name on the suspect list.

"Not Jeff!" Harriet exclaimed before Joe had finished writing the letter *J*.

"We know Marni signed him in to read a book. And that he was here alone before he left the door open to go fight about wizards with Kitty in the Quiet Corner," Joe explained. "That means he had the opportunity."

The CASE of the
MISSING MYSTERY

What? _Magical Moon_ is MISSING
Where? _Rare Reads_
When? _Between 3 and 4 pm_
Who? SUSPECTS:
        Jeff

Harriet twisted her hands together. "I know Jeff can get overexcited sometimes, but he's one of our most passionate readers. Do you really think he could have done this?"

Joe went over to the Rare Reads table to look at the small pile of books someone had left there. Most of them looked like regular library books, but the fancy leather cover of the one on top gave it away as part of the Rare Reads collection. *The Wild World of Wizarding* was printed in a fancy, old-fashioned-type font on the front. Frank walked over to the clipboard hanging by the door.

"Yup," he said, reading the last line. "Marni signed Jeff in to read *The Wild World of Wizarding* at three thirty-five p.m. He was here reading it right before arguing with Kitty, and he could have run back in to steal *Magical Moon* on his way out."

"But Jeff loves the library," Harriet said.

"Which would have made him even angrier when he lost the Reading Robe," Joe suggested.

"We all saw how upset he was when you took it away and kicked him out," Frank added. "He even threatened that you'd be sorry for it. That gives him a reason *why* he might have done it."

"Right. His motive could have been revenge," Joe said.

"Jeff." Harriet moaned. "How could you?"

"It looks bad, but there are a lot of people in the library," Frank cautioned. "It's still possible someone else could have snuck into the Rare Reads room while Jeff left it unattended. A good detective covers every angle."

Joe examined the open door of the empty display case. "We've covered the *W*s, but what about *how* the suspect did it?"

"That case should be locked tight!" Harriet insisted. "We only open the special cases for kids if they sign in to read one of the big three, and no one can lay a finger on them without special gloves *and* me or a Junior Librarian supervising them."

Joe double-checked the clipboard and shook his head. "No one has signed in to read *Magical Moon* all week. There's no reason for the case to be unlocked."

"And there's no sign of anyone trying to break into it either." Frank leaned in for a closer look at the lock. The glass around it gleamed like it had been freshly polished. There was barely even a fingerprint on it. "Whoever did it, it's possible they may have taken more than just the book. There aren't even any scratches on the lock. It must have been opened normally with the key."

Harriet sucked in a deep breath. "It couldn't have been. Marni and I are the only ones here with a key to the key cabinet. You don't think Jeff broke into the key cabinet too, do you?"

"Let's find out!" Frank marched out the door toward the front desk, with Joe and Harriet right behind him.

"Hi, bookworms!" Joe said to the earthworms crawling around in the giant dirt-filled aquarium behind the front desk. There had to be hundreds of them tunneling around different parts of the tank.

Harriet ran a special class called Waste Not with Worms: Team Up with Earthworms to Turn Garbage into Compost. Kids could even bring kitchen scraps from home or banana peels and apple cores from their snacks to drop into the tank for the worms to eat.

"The squiggly wigglies get to chow down all day long, and they have a view of the entire library."

Joe sighed with admiration. "Those worms have it made."

"Too bad they can't tell us who took *Magical Moon*," Frank complained as Harriet pulled out her key ring and unlocked the cabinet behind the desk where she kept all the keys the library staff used. The key chain labeled RARE READS was right on the hook where it was supposed to be, with the keys for the door and cabinets all dangling from the metal ring.

Frank scratched his head. "Huh? How did the thief get the display case open without a key?"

"I can't believe someone would do this," Harriet moaned. "I'm counting on you boys to help me find the missing book before the council meeting."

"We're going to solve this crime and save the library!" Joe assured the librarian as she walked away with her head down. "I hope," he mumbled to Frank after she left. "I don't understand how someone could get the case open without the key."

Frank shrugged helplessly. "Let's go interview some of the other kids to see if anyone saw anything that might give us a clue," he said, taking the clue book from Joe.

They were just about to head back down the aisle when someone tapped Frank on the shoulder. When he turned around, Marni was standing there, staring down at her fuzzy Winnie-the-Pooh feet.

"I—I—" she stammered, struggling to get the words out. "I need to confess something."

Joe and Frank whipped around to look at each other. Was the case about to solve itself?

"You do?" they asked Marni at the same time.

Marni cast a guilty glance up at the SUPPORT THE JUNIOR PUBLIC LIBRARY sign and nodded. "It's my fault the town council is going to close the library."

Chapter 5

READING BETWEEN THE LINES

"You're the one who stole the book from the Rare Reads room?" Joe asked Marni. "But why?"

Marni took a step back. "What are you talking about?"

"You just confessed to stealing the book," Frank said. "Why did you do it?"

Marni gawked at him. "I didn't confess to stealing the book! I would never take anything from the library! I don't know what I'll do if it closes."

Joe raised his eyebrow. "But you said it was your fault the library might close."

"It is!" Marni insisted.

"How is it your fault if you didn't do anything wrong?" Frank asked.

"But I did do something wrong! I did something awful! I didn't steal *Magical Moon*, but—" Marni paused. "I kind of maybe cleaned the Rare Reads room earlier."

Joe blinked. "That . . . doesn't sound so awful."

"And forgot to lock all the display cases when I was done."

"Ohhhhh," Frank and Joe uttered at the same time.

"So *that's* how the crook got away with the book without the keys," Frank said.

"Yeah," Marni said meekly. "I'm the worst person ever."

"Making a mistake doesn't make you a bad person," Joe told her. "Admitting it and trying to help even makes you a good one."

Marni looked unconvinced.

"Your cleaning also explains why the case was so spotless," Frank said. "Well, that's one mystery solved, but we still don't know who took the book. And unless we find out soon, the library is doomed!"

"Is there anything else I can do to help?" Marni asked hopefully.

"Did you see anything suspicious between the time you signed Jeff into Rare Reads and when you discovered that *Magical Moon* was missing?" Joe asked.

"Just Jeff yelling at Kitty about wizards, but you all saw that too," she replied.

Frank slapped the clue book. "That leads us right back to our first lead."

"It's interrogation time," Joe said, heading for the exit.

Frank and Joe raced toward Jeff's house on their bikes. Jeff lived right down the street from the Hardys, and the boys figured that was the best place to look for him. They were right. When they rang the doorbell, Jeff was the one who answered.

He scowled at them through the cracked-open front door. "What do *you* want?"

Jeff might have lost the Reading Robe, but he wasn't entirely robeless. He was wearing an old fuzzy bathrobe, along with a pair of black socks.

Jeff inched farther behind the door. "Why are you looking at me like that?"

"As if you don't know," said Joe accusingly.

Jeff started to turn pink. "It's bad enough that Harriet took my robe away. You don't have to make me feel worse about it."

"You're the one who threatened revenge," Frank reminded him. "Only what you did hurts everyone, not just Harriet."

Jeff bit his lip. "I just said that stuff because I was angry. I didn't mean it. And I told you not to make me feel worse. I know I messed up."

Joe planted his hands on his hips. "So you admit it?"

"It's not like I can deny it. Why do you keep rubbing it in?"

"We have our confession," Joe declared.

"Now we need the book." Frank shoved his palm out at Jeff. "The town council is going to close the library for sure if it isn't returned right away."

Jeff squinted at Frank. "The book?"

"Hand it over," Joe ordered.

"Hand *what* over?"

"The book you took," Frank said.

"I didn't take any book."

"Then what did you just confess to?" Joe asked.

"Leaving the Rare Reads door open, what else?" Jeff snapped. "But I don't know why you need a confession. You were there when it happened. Now who took what book?"

Frank threw his hands up in frustration. "The one that just happened to vanish from Rare Reads when you were on your way out of the library after threatening Harriet with revenge!"

"I didn't take it!" Jeff shouted, then looked down at his socks. "I know I should have put it back, but I'd never take it. It wasn't even that good."

"Wasn't that good?" Frank did a double take. "*Magical Moon* is one of the most famous classics ever!"

Jeff gasped so loudly it sounded almost like a shriek. "*Magical Moon* is gone?!"

"Of course *Magical Moon* is gone," Joe said. "What book did you think we were talking about?"

"The one I signed in to read. *The Wild World of Wizarding*," Jeff proclaimed as if it were obvious. "I know we're supposed to sign rare books back in when we're done, but I was so upset after Harriet kicked me out, I ran right out of the library without thinking." He took a deep breath. "It was irresponsible of me to leave it out on the Rare Reads table like that."

Frank eyed him suspiciously. "So you didn't sneak back into Rare Reads on your way out and steal *Magical Moon*?"

Jeff crossed his arms. "Reigning Readers don't steal books!"

"But you're no longer the Reigning Reader," Joe reminded him.

"Once a Reigning Reader, always a Reigning Reader," Jeff said proudly. "It's a way of life. You know that, Frank."

"It is hard to imagine someone who cares about the library as much as we do trying to harm it," Frank conceded.

"I thought that's exactly what we were imagining," Joe said, confused.

Frank considered it for a moment. "Well, he was around *when* and he definitely had a *why*, but he also has a pretty good *why not*."

This time Joe threw his hands up. "Why does everyone keep confessing, then un-confessing?"

"How would I steal it anyway?" Jeff asked. "The case is locked tight."

Frank's eyes widened. "You don't know about the unlocked case?"

"What unlocked case?" Jeff responded.

"He could be pretending not to know about the unlocked case," Joe suggested.

"I don't know, Joe." Frank rested his chin on his fist. "If he really did leave the library before Marni discovered the book was missing, it would make sense why he doesn't seem to know about the unlocked case *or* the theft. The timing of it all is still super suspicious, but there were plenty of other people in the library who could have snuck into Rare Reads after he left."

"I guess we don't have any real proof." Joe studied Jeff. "And he does seem to be telling the truth."

"Of course I'm telling the truth! I know I can get worked up sometimes—I just love books so much! I'd never intentionally do anything to hurt the junior library." Jeff looked like he was holding back tears. "If I hadn't left the door to Rare Reads open, none of this would have happened. If the library closes, I'll have ruined things for everyone." He gulped. "And I might never get to wear the Reading Robe ever again."

Frank and Joe looked from Jeff back to each other. They believed him. Which meant they were out of suspects.

Chapter 6

WORM'S-EYE VIEW

The first thing Frank and Joe did after leaving Jeff's house and returning home was call all the used bookstores and antique shops in town to see if anyone had tried to sell the stolen book. They hadn't. The boys even looked online to see if anyone was trying to sell it on one of the big auction or rare-book sites. They didn't get any hits there, either.

"That book is worth a fortune," Frank said as they sat down to eat. "If the crook's *why* isn't revenge like we first thought, then making money sure could be."

"If it is, they haven't tried cashing in yet," Joe replied. "Unless they planned the crime in advance and already had a buyer lined up."

Frank shook his head. "Not unless they were psychic. There's no way they could have known that Jeff was going to leave that door open—"

"Or that Marni was going to leave the case open," Joe finished Frank's thought for him. "If they hadn't both goofed, the thief never would have been able to get their hands on it. Whoever did this got lucky. This was a crime of opportunity."

Joe opened the clue book to their suspect list. Both Marni's and Jeff's names were crossed off. "Okay, so who else had an opportunity?"

Frank frowned. "Only, like, all twenty kids who were in the library."

Joe closed the book again. "I think it's time for us to move on to the next item on our detective to-do list—surveillance. Criminals like to return to the scene of the crime, and if it was one of the

The CASE of
MISSING MYS___
What? *Magical Moon*
Where? *Rare Reads*
When? *Between 3 and*
Who? SUSPECTS:
Jeff
Marini

kids, then they could be a library regular. We can watch to see who's acting suspicious."

"We can keep our eyes peeled while I'm doing my Junior Librarian duties when the library opens in the morning, but we can't be there all day or watch the whole place at once," Frank pointed out. "Even with Harriet, Marni, and me all working, someone still snuck into Rare Reads without any of us noticing."

"We may not be able to watch everything at once." Joe grinned as he picked up the phone. "But I know who can."

A half hour later, they were back inside the closed library, standing in front of the worm-farm aquarium with Harriet.

"I want to do everything I can to find *Magical Moon*, but I don't understand how my bookworms are supposed to help." Harriet tossed in some kitchen scraps for the worms to munch on. "I know you said they have a view of the whole library, but you can't interview an invertebrate!"

"Nope, but we can still enlist their help," Joe assured her. "To make sure our surveillance doesn't miss anything, we're going to need another set of eyes. Worm eyes!"

"Well, worms don't technically have eyes," Frank informed Joe. "They have special receptor cells that let them sense whether it's light or dark."

"And that's going to help us how?" Harriet asked.

"It's not!" Joe replied cheerily, pulling out the tiny remote camera they'd brought along. "This is! We don't need *actual* worm eyes to get a worm's-eye view."

"We may not be able to watch the whole library at once, but our remote cam can." Frank told the librarian about Joe's plan as his brother climbed up on a step stool to place the camera inside the worm tank. "Disguised under a layer of dirt, no one will even know it's there. If anyone is behaving suspiciously or tries to steal anything else, we'll be sure to see it."

"Worms!" Joe exclaimed. "The perfect spies!"

Harriet chuckled. "I never thought my book-worms would become undercover detectives!"

Joe climbed back down and tested the camera with an app on his tablet. "Thanks for letting us back in after hours."

"Thank *you* boys for trying to crack this case." Harriet glanced at the SUPPORT THE JUNIOR PUBLIC LIBRARY sign. "I've been talking to everyone I know to make sure we have tons of people telling the town council to keep the library open, but unless we get that book back, I don't think we have a chance."

Back at home, Joe checked the remote cam on his tablet one last time to make sure everything was working properly before going to bed. There was just enough light in the dark library for the camera to get an image. Right as he was about to turn it off, a shadow passed in front of the worm tank.

REC ●

Joe blinked to make sure he wasn't seeing things. Nope. There was a person sneaking into the BJPL!

"Get over here, bro!" he called to Frank. "The worms see something!"

Frank ran into Joe's room to look at the screen. His mouth dropped open. "The library's been closed for hours. No one should be in there."

"Tell that to them." Joe pointed to the cloaked figured creeping past the front desk toward the mystery aisle. They were wearing a hood, so there was no way to see the person's face.

"They must have broken in," Frank observed. "What if they're trying to steal more books?"

The boys held their breath as the figure glanced back over their shoulder, then reached out toward one of the shelves.

Only they weren't stealing a book. They were putting one back.

JUDGE A CROOK BY ITS COVER

"Thieves take things!" Frank watched wide-eyed as the hooded figure neatly aligned the spines of the books next to the one they'd just put back. "They don't return them!"

"Or tidy up!" Joe added.

"It doesn't make any sense." Frank stared intently at the screen. "Who would break into a library to return a book?"

"Maybe it was really overdue?"

"Or maybe they're feeling guilty after stealing it," Frank said seriously. "Let's watch to see where they go next. Maybe they'll put *Magical Moon* back too!"

The reverse thief didn't head for the Rare Reads room, though. They hurried right back toward the front of the library, looking around nervously as they went. As the person got closer, the boys could tell they weren't wearing just any old hooded cloak. It was a Reading Robe!

Just as the Reading Robed perpetrator passed the front desk, the person glanced at the worm tank—and directly into the worm cam hidden under the dirt. It was only for a second, but there was just enough light for the boys to make out the face beneath the hood.

"The Big Bad Wolf?" Joe asked, squinting at the screen.

Sure enough, the person was wearing a mask that looked like a wolf's face. They were even carrying a little basket, where they must have hidden the

book they'd returned. Along with the red robe, they looked like a combination of the Big Bad Wolf and Little Red Riding Hood from the fairy tale.

Frank snapped his fingers. "There's only one person I know who would disguise themself as a character from a story to sneak into a library."

"Marni," Joe growled as their no-longer-nameless perp vanished from view.

"If we rush, we can catch her before she makes it back to her house." Frank was already sprinting out of the room and down the stairs, with Joe close behind him, carrying the tablet.

They ran past their dad, Fenton Hardy, who was sitting on the porch reading a newspaper, and hopped on their bikes.

"Mystery emergency!" Joe called to their dad, dropping the tablet into the bike's basket and strapping on his bike helmet as he spoke.

Mr. Hardy was Bayport's most famous private investigator. The boys had told him all about the case at dinner, and he knew how important it was. The Bayport Junior Public Library was at stake, and if there was one thing Fenton Hardy loved almost as much as his sons and solving mysteries, it was reading. Besides, as a detective himself, he understood that sometimes a big break in a case was more important than bedtime.

"Clues can't wait," Mr. Hardy said, peering over his newspaper. "Can I give you a ride?"

"Thanks, Dad, but we're only going a couple of blocks to Marni's house." Joe pointed down the well-lit, quiet street.

Frank flipped on his bike's flashing safety lights. "We'll stay in the bike lane and follow all the bike safety rules like you taught us."

Mr. Hardy looked at his watch. "In that case, I think we can grant a one-hour emergency bedtime exemption as long as you—"

"Follow the clues *and* the rules," Frank and Joe recited at the same time, finishing one of their dad's favorite sayings for him.

Mr. Hardy smiled. "Go get that book, boys." He set down his newspaper and stood up. "And I'll follow behind you in the car just in case you need backup."

The boys were used to their dad sometimes tagging along on their cases. They knew he would still let them investigate on their own and only bother them if there was trouble they couldn't handle.

"Marni must have been lying to us earlier," Frank said to Joe as they raced side by side toward Marni's house. "She was totally *where when*. She was by herself in Rare Reads when she claimed she found *Magical Moon* gone."

"When she really could have been the one to take

it!" Joe replied. "Telling everyone it was stolen could have been an act to cover her tracks and keep us from suspecting she's the thief."

Frank pedaled harder. "Pretending to be so upset when she confessed to leaving the case unlocked could have been part of the act too. She could have left it unlocked on purpose."

"But if she did, why would she steal one book only to sneak back in to return another?" Joe wondered.

"Let's ask her." Frank skidded his bike to a stop just as Marni turned the corner on her skateboard.

She wasn't wearing the Reading Robe anymore and had taken off the wolf mask, so they could see her face clearly now. She almost tumbled off her skateboard when she saw the Hardys waiting for her. She hopped off in time to keep from wiping out, but the board went flying and landed right at Joe's feet. Marni froze. For a second it looked like she might run, but she must have realized it was pointless. Her shoulders slumped.

"Um, what are you guys doing here?"

"Nothing much, just catching you trying to get

away after breaking into the library." Frank tapped his temple. "We've got eyes everywhere."

Joe wiggled his finger. "Worm eyes."

"Um, technically worms don't have eyes," Marni said.

"That's what I told him!" said Frank.

"They're metaphorical eyes!" Joe held out the tablet with the worm-cam live feed for her to see. "We hid a remote camera in the worm farm and caught you in the act."

"Only we aren't quite sure what you were in the act of doing," Frank admitted.

"What was the book you returned?" Joe glared at Marni. "Was it one of the ones you stole?"

"I didn't steal any books! I already told you guys I'd never take anything from the library."

"We're more concerned with what you didn't tell us," Frank said.

"I guess what I meant was that I'd never take anything from the library *on purpose*." Marni hesitated. "I—"

The boys leaned in closer.

"I did take a book," Marni whispered, her chin dropping to her chest.

Joe was leaning so far forward, it looked like he might fall over.

"Just not that book," she said.

Frank and Joe both instantly slouched as if they'd been deflated.

"So there was more than one stolen book?" Frank asked.

"I didn't mean to steal it!" Marni insisted. "I was so flustered after everything that happened earlier, I got one of the checked-in books from my cart mixed up with the books I checked out for me. When I got home and opened my backpack, I realized I'd taken a mystery that was supposed to go back on the shelf. I was afraid if Harriet or you guys found out, I'd be accused of stealing *Magical Moon*, too."

"So you weren't covering up a crime?" Joe asked.

"Just another embarrassing mistake." Marni sighed. "Even if Harriet believed me that I took it by accident, I already messed up big-time once today by leaving the case unlocked. If I got caught botching something else, I could lose my Junior Librarian job. Harriet showed me where she keeps an emergency front door key hidden outside of the library. I thought if I could borrow it to secretly return the other book, no one would know, and I wouldn't get in trouble for losing track of things. Or worse, blamed for stealing *Magical Moon*, too!"

Frank and Joe eyed her closely. It was obvious that Marni felt guilty, but that didn't mean she *was* guilty.

"It wouldn't make much sense for you to return one book and not the other," Frank acknowledged.

"I guess it's a good thing the worms were watching. Otherwise you might not believe me."

Joe ran his hand down his face. "But if Jeff didn't take it and you didn't take it, who took it?"

"I wish I knew. If the town council votes tomorrow to shut down the library, I'll lose my job that way too. The library is the only place I can really be myself—"

"And sometimes Winnie-the-Pooh, the Big Bad

Wolf, and about a hundred other characters," Joe reminded Marni.

Marni frowned. "It's my happy place. I don't know what I'll do without it!"

"I think Marni is guilty of the same thing Jeff is," Frank said. "Being a little careless."

Joe handed the skateboard back to Marni. "Which isn't a crime."

"And we're out of clues," Frank said.

"Maybe we can try to convince the council to delay the vote," Joe suggested. "Tom wants to save the library too. Maybe he can get the rest of the council to give us more time."

"I have something else to return too." Marni reached into her bag and pulled out an expanding file folder that looked like a cross between a large envelope and a small accordion. It was about an inch thick, and the flap was sealed neatly shut with a strip of tape. "I found this under the table in the Quiet Corner when I was cleaning up yesterday. It must have fallen out of Councilman Hinkley's briefcase when Jeff knocked into him. I wasn't sure if I should leave it at the library or try to give it back to him. If you're going to see him anyway, maybe you could give it to him."

Frank held out his hand to take the folder from Marni. He could see the Bayport Town Council seal stamped in one of the corners, along with a separate typed label in the center. "This will give us a good reason to go see him."

"And maybe for returning it, we'll get some brownie points to help our cause," Joe added.

"Um, Joe." Frank pointed to the label and gave his bike bell an enthusiastic *DING*. "I think we found our next clue!"

PUTT-PUTT PLOT TWIST

Joe squinted at the folder in Frank's hand. "We have?"

"This is the budget proposal for the golf course renovation," Frank said excitedly.

"But the file folder is sealed. It even says it's private." Joe pointed to a bright red stamp in the other corner that read CONFIDENTIAL. "It would be wrong to snoop inside town files without Councilman Hinkley's permission."

"We don't have to." Frank pointed to three words

printed under the report's title in smaller letters. "The clue is printed right here."

Joe leaned in for a closer look and read the words aloud. "'By Bonnie Becker.' Of course! If there's anyone with a *why* to sabotage the BJPL before the town council vote, it's her!"

"Yup," Frank agreed. "She's the one who wrote this report. I don't have to open the folder to guess that she wants all the money that would have gone to the BJPL to go to the golf course."

Joe's shoulders slumped. "There's only one problem with that theory. Councilwoman Becker wasn't at the library *when*. She couldn't have stolen *Magical Moon* because she wasn't there."

"Nope." Frank grinned. "But her daughter was."

Joe perked back up instantly. "Kitty totally had the opportunity to steal it! She left the Quiet Corner right after Harriet came over to tell Jeff to quiet down. She could have easily snuck into Rare Reads to take *Magical Moon* from the unlocked case while we were talking to Councilman Hinkley."

"Yeah, because I forgot to lock it," Marni

mumbled, tugging on the strap of her backpack.

"You may have opened the case, but we're going to close it." Frank held up the folder. "And we're going to start first thing tomorrow morning."

Frank and Joe were back on their bikes and headed for the golf course as soon as they'd finished breakfast. Frank had the folder and Joe had the clue book. A new name was written under Suspects: *Kitty Becker*.

"I hear Kitty talking about practicing for the next golf tournament all the time," Frank said as they pulled up to the Bayport Public Golf Course. "I bet we'll find her on the course!"

The boys locked up their bikes and headed into the clubhouse. One of the first things they saw were the Beckers' adult and junior tournament trophies from last year. They were in a display case along with framed copies of articles from the newspaper and a photo of the mother-daughter duo side by side, holding up their matching trophies. They'd both signed the photo. Councilwoman Becker's signature had huge fancy loops and swirls. There were a bunch of

trophies from other tournaments too, and when they looked closely at the winners' names, it seemed like Councilwoman Becker had won more than anyone else. There were also framed pictures of a lot of the course's most prominent golfers, including the mayor and most of the other council members, even Tom.

"Practically the whole town council loves golf." Joe groaned. "How are we ever going to get them to vote for the library over the golf course?"

"They're not voting for just one or the other," Frank reminded him. "They're deciding how much money to give to each. If we get that book back, we can convince them to keep the library open without hurting the golf course."

Joe marched toward the door leading back outside to the golf course. "We better find Kitty quick."

It wasn't Kitty Becker they found first, though. It was her mom.

"Out of the way!" Councilwoman Becker shouted at Joe and Frank while pounding her fist on the horn of her golf cart.

"Eek!" Joe cried as he saw the cart barreling

toward them, and both boys jumped aside just in time to keep from getting run over.

"Ack!" Frank squawked.

"Let's follow that cart, bro!"

The Hardys took off after the golf cart. They didn't have far to run. It pulled to a stop at the course's first hole. The councilwoman, who was dressed in perfectly pressed, perfectly clean white pants, a polo shirt, and a visor, hopped out of the driver's seat and walked to the back of the cart, where her clubs were.

"Excuse me, Councilwoman!" Joe shouted. "We need to talk to you!"

She stopped and looked at them. "Is it about donating money to my reelection campaign?"

"Um, no," Joe replied.

"Sorry then, no time." She didn't sound very sorry at all as she selected a club from her golf bag. "These holes won't play themselves, and I have to get to the office."

"It's about town business, though," Frank declared. "And it's important."

Councilwoman Becker crossed her arms and glared at him. "It better be. I golf and I govern. In that order. If you're going to hold up my game, it better be a matter of life and death."

"It is," Joe shot back. "The life of the Bayport Junior Public Library."

The councilwoman gave a humph as she got ready to tee off. "Nothing to discuss. That pricey book your librarian lost seals it. As far as I'm concerned, the matter is closed. And so is the library."

"You can't just close the library!" Frank cried. "That book wasn't lost. It was stolen!"

"Sure I can," she said casually, lining up her shot. "Books are a waste of paper. We're going to spend the town's money on something that actually matters to people. Golf."

"What if we told you someone sabotaged the library to make it easier for the council to vote to close it?" Joe asked just as she was about to hit the ball.

Councilwoman Becker was caught so off guard that she sliced the ball right into the bushes. She whipped around to face him. "Don't you know not to talk when someone is teeing off? I'm calling a mulligan."

"Who is Mulligan?" Joe asked. "Is he involved in the vote?"

The councilwoman rolled her eyes. "A mulligan is a golf do-over. A free extra shot on the scorecard."

She pulled a new ball from her pocket. "It means I get a second chance. Unlike your library."

Frank crossed his arms. "What if we can prove the person doing the sabotage has ties to the town council?"

She was about to swing again, but stopped mid-stroke.

"That would sure cause quite a scandal," Frank said. "Especially if it was your daughter who did it."

Councilwoman Becker suddenly snickered. "You think Kitty stole that book the library lost track of?"

"You could have even told her to do it to make sure the council voted to give the money the library needs to the golf course," Joe speculated.

"*My daughter*, Kitty?" The councilwoman's snicker had turned into a full-on laugh. "Took orders from *me*? To sabotage the library?"

"What's so funny?" Joe demanded.

The councilwoman smirked and pointed her club toward a grove of trees off to the side of the course. "Why don't you go ask her?"

In the direction she was pointing, they could see

Kitty sitting at the base of a tree with a sketchbook in her hands, occasionally looking up at the branches. Her golf clubs were tossed to the side.

"Now stop wasting my time, and go waste hers." The councilwoman turned her attention back to the golf ball. "Not that she needs any help."

As the boys marched off to confront Kitty, they could hear the councilwoman muttering something to herself about trees being almost as worthless as books.

As they got closer, they could see that Kitty was sketching something.

"Hello, Kitty," Joe said ominously as they approached.

Kitty turned and smiled warmly. "Oh, hi, Joe! Hi, Frank! What are you doing here?"

The boys looked at each other. That wasn't the greeting they were expecting.

"We're here to interrogate you!" Frank announced. "Um, we think."

"Interrogate me?" Kitty lowered her sketchbook. Frank could see that she'd been making a detailed sketch of a tiny bud on one of the tree branches. "Wait, does this have to do with someone stealing *Magical Moon*?"

"What do you know about it?" Joe demanded.

"Just that it was stolen yesterday. My mom told me the town council had a special meeting about it. It was all over the local news, too." Kitty suddenly dropped her sketchbook to the side. "Wait! You don't think I had anything to do with it, do you?"

"You and your mom are Bayport golf legends."

Frank stomped a foot on the perfectly mowed grass. "If anyone benefits from the golf course getting renovated, it's you. The library closing means even more money for the course."

Kitty staggered backward with her mouth open. "But I love the library! I've been trying to convince my mom not to shut it down!"

"You—" Joe did a double take. "You what?"

"I mean, sure, I like golf well enough, but I don't care about a fancy clubhouse, new golf carts, or any of the extra stuff my mom wants to add." Kitty looked horrified. "She even wants to expand the course!"

"And you think that's a bad thing?"

"Um, yeah! A bigger course would mean using tons of extra water *and* cutting down more trees!" She gently patted the tree she'd been sketching. "That would be a violation of my conservation pledge to the Environment Club."

Kitty pointed to a button on her golf bag that read READ, RECYCLE, REPEAT. "I mean—" And then she pointed to her shirt. With her sketchbook by her side, the boys could read it clearly now. It said

I ♥ TREES. They had to admit to themselves that it didn't look like the kind of shirt someone who wanted to tear down trees would wear.

"I've got a whole speech prepared to give at the council meeting tonight," Kitty continued. "I'm going to ask them to split the money between the library and eco-friendly water conservation upgrades to the golf course. That way everyone benefits, even the trees! Harriet helped me with it in the library's writing workshop."

"She did?" Frank asked, sounding a lot less confident than he had a minute earlier.

"And I've got an airtight alibi, too." Kitty cocked her eyebrow. "There were people around the whole time I was at the library yesterday. There's no way I could have snuck into Rare Reads without someone seeing me. A bunch of different people witnessed Jeff come out to argue with me about wizards, and I walked past at least five onlookers after I left the Quiet Corner. I can give you a list of names if you want to check my alibi. I can account for my whole timeline during the crime."

"You can?" Joe gave a sad look at his clue book.

"You guys may be detectives, but I've read half the books in the mystery section," she said proudly. "I know the lingo."

Joe slowly drew a line through Kitty's name under *Suspects*. The space below it was blank.

Kitty looked over his shoulder at the clue book. "If you boys were expecting this interrogation to end with a case-breaking revelation, you're going to need a better cliff-hanger."

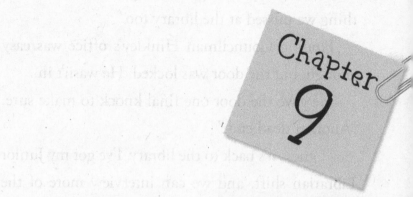

Chapter
9

AN OPEN BOOK

"The town council meeting is tonight, and we aren't any closer to solving the crime," Frank said as they left the golf course.

Joe held up the clue book. "And we're out of suspects. Who do we talk to next?"

"Let's head for town hall." Frank hopped back onto his bike. "We can return Councilman Tom's file folder and see if there's any way to delay the vote to give us more time."

Joe started pedaling. "He might have seen something we missed at the library too."

Finding Councilman Hinkley's office was easy enough, but the door was locked. He wasn't in.

Joe gave the door one final knock to make sure. "Another dead end."

"I guess it's back to the library. I've got my Junior Librarian shift, and we can interview more of the kids who were there yesterday to see if we can stir up some more clues."

"And we can check the worm cam!" Joe gave his bike bell an enthusiastic *DING*.

He was less enthusiastic a few hours later. "The worms didn't see anything interesting."

"None of the kids I talked to did either." Frank looked over at Harriet, who was frantically making phone calls, rallying library supporters to show up at the council meeting. She'd been either on the phone, sending emails, or chewing her nails all day. "We're almost out of time. What are we going to do?"

Joe's stomach grumbled as he eyed a half-eaten apple in the bookworm tank. "Get dinner. The bookworms have been chowing down all day, and it's making my tummy jealous."

"The book crook is still on the loose, and all my brother can think about is food!"

Joe rubbed his belly. "You know how I feel about detecting on an empty stomach."

They talked about the case all through dinner and dessert without getting any closer to figuring out who took the book. Joe had the clue book open in front of him. The only thing he'd added to it were ketchup stains. The folder they had to return to Councilman Hinkley was next to it.

"We have to leave soon for the town council meeting." Frank stabbed his fork into a barely touched slice of cherry pie. "It looks like we might have to go without knowing whodunit."

"But we can't let Harriet and the library down!" Joe banged his fist on the table.

"Watch out!" Frank cried.

Joe hadn't been paying attention to the glass of chocolate milk next to him, and when he thumped

the table, it started to tip over. Frank and Joe both reached for it, but neither of them were quick enough. The chocolatey brown liquid spilled all over Councilman Hinkley's folder!

The ink on the front instantly started to smear, including the big red letters that said CONFIDENTIAL.

Frank grabbed the folder and tried to shake the liquid off. Some of it had already soaked through. "I don't want to snoop in anyone's private files, but if we don't open that folder, all the papers inside could be ruined!"

"Ruining important town council files won't help us convince them to keep the library open." Joe gripped the table as Frank tore open the sealed flap and pulled out a stapled document.

The chocolate milk had already started to stain the papers inside, but it wasn't too bad. They could still read the title page easily enough through the brown blotches.

Golf Course Renovation Proposal
Confidential Report
For Council Members Only
Prepared by B. Becker

Under that, it listed the names of each council member.

Frank dabbed at the chocolate stains with a napkin and then started shaking the report to dry it. That was when a damp letter-size envelope fell out from between the pages and drifted to the floor.

Joe bent down to pick up the envelope. Not snooping wasn't an option. He could instantly read the neat handwriting on the back side of the envelope without having to try. The first line made him growl.

"'Don't worry about the Bayport Junior Public Lemons,'" Joe read aloud.

The second line made him so angry, he couldn't even repeat it. He handed the note to Frank instead.

Frank understood why when he read it for himself.

No one on the council will trust the library with the town's money when we're done. And they'll never suspect me. Brand-new golf course, here we come!

Joe balled his hands into fists. "They're talking about sabotaging the library!"

"The file was sealed when Marni gave it to us, and copies of the exact same report were given to everyone on the town council too." Frank looked from the envelope back to the chocolate-stained document. "The note could have been written by anyone and accidentally gotten stuck to one of the reports. The glue must have come unstuck when it got wet."

The envelope was the kind with a clear plastic window, and they could see there wasn't anything inside.

Frank flipped the envelope over. "There's more on the other side!"

Joe leaned in closer. The ink on this side was blue instead of black, and the handwriting was different.

"And it's written by someone else," Joe observed. "They must have passed the note back and forth!"

The brothers read the note silently.

I don't want to know how you do it,
but I'm trusting you to get those votes.
No mulligans on this one.

"It's a conspiracy!" Frank snarled. "I bet one of these people is our thief."

"The handwriting on this side isn't just different." Joe poked his finger at the fancy loops and swirls. "It's distinctive!"

"Those aren't the only distinctive marks on it." Frank flipped the envelope back over and held it up to the window. "And I don't mean the chocolate stains."

Early evening sunlight poked through a group of tiny holes in the corner. It almost looked like it had been stabbed by lots of pointy little dots.

"Let's get to that council meeting." Frank grinned and headed for the door. "We have everything we need to catch our book thief!"

THE HARDY BOYS—and
YOU!

DO YOU KNOW WHO TOOK THE MISSING BOOK FROM
the Bayport Junior Public Library?

Think like a Hardy Boy to crack the case. Write your answers down on a piece of paper. Or just turn the page to find out!

1. Frank and Joe suspected Jeff, Marni, Kitty, and her mom, Councilwoman Becker, but they all seemed to be innocent. Who else could have taken the book?

2. The holes in the corner of the envelope Frank and Joe found gave them the final clue they needed to solve the case. Can you think of what could have made them?

3. If you had your own private Rare Reads room to show off all your favorite books, what are the top three books you would put in it?

DOG-EARED DETECTION

"We saw that same handwriting earlier today at the golf course," Frank said as he ran out the door. "On the framed photo signed by Councilwoman Becker!"

Joe was right behind him. "She's guilty!"

"Actually, I think this proves Councilwoman Becker *didn't* steal the book," Frank replied, jumping back onto his bike. "She wrote that she didn't want to know the details. But she was definitely conspiring with the person who did."

Joe leapt onto his bike as well. "But the envelope doesn't have any names and everyone on the council got the same report. Anyone Becker knows could have written the note on the other side, and the envelope just got stuck to this one, like you said."

"Not just anyone. Those weren't just holes in the corner of the envelope."

Joe did a bunny hop on his bike as it dawned on him. "They were teeth marks!"

The boys pedaled as fast as they could toward the town hall. It was already packed when they got there. Outside, a bunch of kids and adults were holding SAVE THE LIBRARY signs. There was even a local news truck there to film the meeting, and a few police officers. Inside, it was standing room only. Frank and Joe pushed their way toward the front of the room, where Harriet, Kitty, and a bunch of other BJPL supporters were seated. Marni, dressed as Dracula, was right next to Harriet. Next to the librarian was Jeff. Getting kicked out hadn't stopped him from joining Harriet to fight for the library.

There was a sudden *BANG-BANG* from the

stage at the front of the room as Councilwoman Becker slammed her gavel onto the table where all the council members, including Tom Hinkley, were seated. A long tablecloth with the town seal was draped around the table.

"All right, Bayport, let's get this meeting teed off," she announced into the microphone in front of her.

"Good idea," called Joe, pushing his way right up to the table. "We've got some unofficial council business the town needs to know about."

The councilwoman rolled her eyes. "You again. The public will have a chance to make comments before we vote." She looked past Frank to the crowded room behind him. "Now, everyone knows it's an open-and-shut case, but we'll be voting on measures to close the dysfunctional junior library and use the money to renovate the town's beloved public golf course—"

"This comment can't wait," Frank interrupted. "And it's not for you."

"At least not the first one," Joe added, pointing at Tom. "It's for him."

"Me?" Tom squeaked.

The entire room started to murmur.

"The Bayport Junior Public Library isn't dysfunctional," Frank declared. "It was framed to look that way."

"You have quite an imagination, boys." Tom chuckled nervously. "Now, I understand you're upset about the possibility of the library closing. I am too, believe me. But the BJPL lost one of the most valuable books in the whole library system. It's obvious that—"

"That someone stole *Magical Moon* to make the library look bad right before the big vote," Joe interjected before the councilman could finish.

There were gasps from the crowd.

"Th-that's absurd!" Tom stammered. "I was there when it went missing—"

"Exactly," Joe agreed. "You *who*'d the *what when*!"

"I—huh?" Tom blinked in confusion as Joe continued.

"That's detective-speak for: you had the perfect opportunity to steal the book when you walked past the open Rare Reads room on your way into the library yesterday."

"I would never!" Tom shot back. "I'm one of the library's biggest supporters!"

"That's what you want everyone to think." Frank held up the incriminating envelope that had fallen out of the councilman's folder. "It's the perfect cover story to let you sabotage the library without anyone suspecting you. You admit it right here."

"I've never seen that before in my life!" Tom hollered.

Frank ignored the councilman's denial and kept talking. "There's no way you could have known that either the Rare Reads room or the display would be unlocked. That was luck. But this note is evidence that you went to the library with a mission to bring back a negative report to the council, and maybe even plant evidence if you had to."

"Is this true, Tom?" Harriet asked, standing up from her seat.

He shook his head vigorously.

Joe turned to the librarian. "The mess from the books we dropped and all the yelling he heard might have been enough to convince the undecided voters. He even said he had to report those things. But when he saw that everyone was distracted by Jeff arguing with Kitty, it gave him the perfect chance to duck into Rare Reads while no one was paying attention and nab *Magical Moon* undetected."

"Until now," Frank added, glaring at both Tom

Hinkley and Bonnie Becker. The councilwoman had gone silent and was slinking down in her seat.

The council member seated next to Tom Hinkley took off her big, flashy glasses and looked Frank in the eye. The name plaque in front of her read VALENTINA TORRES. "These are very serious allegations, young man."

"They're not serious," Tom snapped. "They're ridiculous! These kids are obviously just upset about the library closing and concocting wild stories to try to save it."

"We're trying to save it, all right," Frank retorted. "And thanks to you, we have the proof we need."

"And thanks to Jeff and Marni," Joe said, smiling at the befuddled library lovers behind him. "Jeff doesn't know it, but he accidentally helped solve the case when he knocked over Councilman Hinkley's briefcase on the way out of the library yesterday."

"I did?" Jeff asked.

Joe held up the folder Marni had found. "The councilman accidentally left this behind."

Councilwoman Torres squinted at the folder.

"What's so special about that? All of us got the same report."

Frank displayed the envelope that had fallen out when Joe spilled the chocolate milk. "I bet all of them didn't have this inside."

"You're saying the evidence is in that envelope?" asked Councilwoman Torres.

"It's not what's in it," Frank said. "It's what's on it."

"That's just an envelope," Tom protested. "It doesn't prove anything."

"Nope, but the notes you and your collaborator wrote on it do." Frank held up the side with the fancy handwriting for Bonnie Becker to see. "Recognize the handwriting, Councilwoman?"

"Me?" she croaked.

Frank pointed to the large loops. "It matches yours exactly."

Kitty hopped up, snatched the envelope from Frank's hand, gave both sides a quick read, then glared up at the stage. "Mom! How could you?!"

"I think there's been a—I—um—" Bonnie

Becker hopped up from her seat and suddenly ran for the door. "Left my golf cart running. Gotta go!"

Councilwoman Torres leaped out of her chair. "You can't leave! What's going on here?" She reached her hand out over the table and down toward Kitty. "Give me that."

Kitty let her take the envelope.

Frank pointed at the writing. "Councilwoman Torres, those notes are proof that Bonnie Becker and Tom Hinkley wrote messages to each other conspiring to shut down the BJPL."

"That's Becky's looping handwriting, all right." The councilwoman flipped it over to read the note on the other side. "The writing here looks kind of familiar, but it's so unremarkable, it could be anyone's."

"Not mine!" Tom shrieked, his voice cracking.

"You may not have left your signature on it, but a companion of yours did." Frank reached out to take the envelope back from Councilwoman Torres. He pointed to the holes in the corner. "These aren't just holes. They're teeth marks."

Councilwoman Torres squinted to get a better look. "They don't look like a person's teeth to me."

"Not a person," Joe informed her. "A pup!"

"A what?" she asked as Tom started squirming in his seat.

Frank fixed him with a stare. "You may have pretended to be on the side of the library, but you also love golf enough to name your dog after it—Mulley is short for mulligan, isn't it?"

Joe flicked the envelope's chewed-up corner. "And we're betting these teeth marks are hers."

There was a playful growling sound from under the table by Tom's feet.

"Right, Mulley?" Joe said, lifting the tablecloth.

There was Mulley in her specially designed puppy pouch. This time the gasps from the crowd were even louder. Mulley had pulled an old book from Tom's briefcase and was using it as a chew toy. The title was clearly visible: *Magical Moon*.

Tom couldn't see what was happening from behind the table. He nervously lifted the tablecloth on his side of the table and let out a whimper.

Joe grinned. "There's no way for you to call a mulligan on this one."

"We're here to make sure your botched shot goes on the town's official scorecard," Frank said with a grin of his own.

Tom jumped out of his seat, but there was nowhere for him to run. A police officer was blocking his way. "You're going to have to come with us, sir."

There were more gasps and murmurs and shouts

from the crowd. The shouts started to turn into a chant.

"SAVE THE LIBRARY! SAVE THE LIBRARY!"

Harriet, Marni, Jeff, and the Hardys all joined in.

"SAVE THE LIBRARY! SAVE THE LIBRARY!"

Councilwoman Torres picked up Bonnie Becker's gavel and pounded it on the table. "We need to restore order to this meeting!"

"Does restoring order include restoring all the money the BJPL needs to stay open?" Frank asked.

"And buying new equipment to replace all the old broken stuff?" Joe added.

"Between the sabotage by our own members and all the support the town has shown for the library, I'm going to say"—she paused to look around the packed room—"yes."

Cheers erupted from the crowd.

Councilwoman Torres turned to the remaining council members. "Does the rest of the council vote to permanently fund the library?"

Every one of them raised their hands immediately.

"It's unanimous!" Frank shouted as Harriet ran

over to wrap him and Joe in a huge bear hug. Marni and Jeff crowded around them, jumping up and down to celebrate.

Frank carefully took the slightly damp copy of *Magical Moon* back from Mulley. "Our prized book might be a little damaged, but at least we have it back."

"And the Bayport Junior Public Library is open for good!" Marni did a celebratory twirl, her vampire cape swooshing through the air.

Harriet pulled Marni and Jeff into the group hug. "I'm going to have to make more robes, because I'm crowning all of you Reigning Readers for life."

"This is the best book day ever!" Jeff exclaimed, wiping away a tear of joy.

"Can you make a robe in size extra small?" Frank lifted Mulley out of the briefcase and gave her head a scratch. "Because Mulley deserves one too!"

"*WOOF!*" the little dog barked in agreement.

Harriet giggled. "You're going to be one posh puppy, Mulley."

Joe flipped open the clue book and wrote the

word *SOLVED*. Frank grabbed the pen and added, *And the Junior Public Library lived happily ever after.*

"There's nothing like a book with a happy ending," Joe said, closing the cover to more cheers from the library-loving friends.

CPSIA information can be obtained
at www.ICGtesting.com
Printed in the USA
BVHW030337310523
665099BV00006B/25

9 781534 476868